AF751606

# KID YOUTUBER
## SORRY, NOT SORRY

MARCUS EMERSON

SCHOLASTIC

*This one's for Gabe . . .*

Scholastic Australia
PO Box 579 Gosford NSW 2250
ABN 11 000 614 577
www.scholastic.com.au

Part of the Scholastic Group
Sydney • Auckland • New York • Toronto • London • Mexico City
New Delhi • Hong Kong • Buenos Aires • Puerto Rico

Published by Emerson Publishing House in 2021.
This edition published by Scholastic Australia in 2024.
Copyright © 2021 Marcus Emerson.

The moral rights of Marcus Emerson have been asserted.

Book design by Marcus Emerson.
Art created digitally in Clip Studio Pro.

All rights reserved. No part of this publication may be reproduced or transmitted in any form or by any means, electronic or mechanical, including photocopying, recording, storage in an information retrieval system, or otherwise, without the prior written permission of the publisher, unless specifically permitted under the Australian Copyright Act 1968 as amended.

ISBN 978-1-76152-534-6

Printed in China by Hang Tai Printing Company Limited.
This product is made of material from well-managed FSC®-certified forests, recycled materials, and other controlled sources.

FSC www.fsc.org MIX Paper | Supporting responsible forestry FSC® C023121

24 25 26 27 28 / 2

## ALSO BY MARCUS EMERSON

**The Diary of a 6th Grade Ninja Novels**
*Diary of a 6th Grade Ninja*
*Diary of a 6th Grade Ninja: Pirate Invasion*
*Diary of a 6th Grade Ninja: Rise of the Red Ninjas*
*Diary of a 6th Grade Ninja: A Game of Chase*
*Diary of a 6th Grade Ninja: Terror at the Talent Show*
*Diary of a 6th Grade Ninja: Buchanan Bandits*
*Diary of a 6th Grade Ninja: Scavengers*
*Diary of a 6th Grade Ninja: Spirit Week Shenanigans*
*Diary of a 6th Grade Ninja: The Scavengers Strike Back*
*Diary of a 6th Grade Ninja: My Worst Frenemy*
*Diary of a 6th Grade Ninja: Beware of the Supermoon*
*Diary of a 6th Grade Ninja: Suckerpunch*

**The Secret Agent 6th Grader Novels**
*Secret Agent 6th Grader*
*Secret Agent 6th Grader: Ice Cold Suckerpunch*
*Secret Agent 6th Grader: Extra Large Soda Jerk*
*Secret Agent 6th Grader: Selfies are Forever*

**The Kid Youtuber Novels**
*Kid Youtuber*
*Kid Youtuber: Hungry for More*
*Kid Youtuber: The Struggle is Real*
*Kid Youtuber: Because Obviously*
*Kid Youtuber: You're Welcome*

**The Ben Braver Novels**
*The Super Life of Ben Braver*
*Ben Braver and the Incredible Exploding Kid*
*Ben Braver and the Vortex of Doom*

**The Recess Warriors Graphic Novels**
*Recess Warriors: Hero is a Four-Letter Word*
*Recess Warriors: Bad Guy is a Two-Word Word*

**Other Illustrated Novels**
*Middle School Ninja: Legacy, The Dodgeball Wars 5 Book Collection, The LOL Collection Volumes 1, 2, & 3*

*Visit MarcusEmerson.com for more info!*

# EPISODE ONE:
# A BIGGER DILL

204 VIEWS 612 FANS

This season's got something for EVERYBODY! Action, adventure, betrayal, and cupcakes, because let's be honest here – who doesn't like cupcakes?

I mean, okay, there are people who SAY they don't like cupcakes, but there's a word for those people...

They're called LIARS.

Anyways, I've been hard at work, busting my be-hind to make this season the best one yet! And I'm not just talkin' about creating content.

For sure, I'm still doing that 24/7, but I'm talkin' about something completely different here – something I'm about to show you, but before I do, I'm required by law to give this warning – the following video has the potential to MAKE YOU FALL IN LOVE WITH ME. If you are susceptible to LOVE AT FIRST SIGHT, then look away... because I just got...

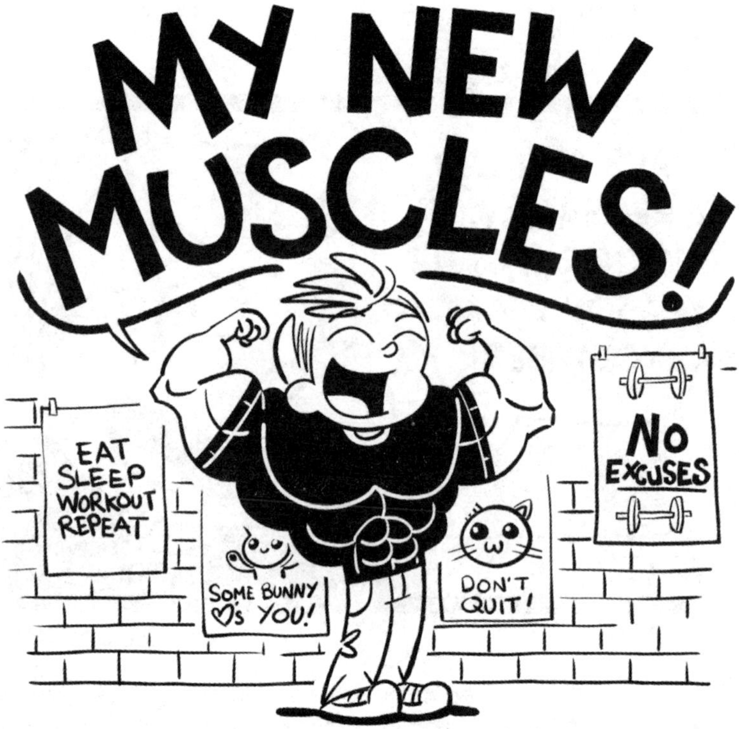


Yup. I've been workin' out since last season, and I've become more shredded than a taco salad!

I don't know why I'm surprised – I'm naturally talented at a whole buncha stuff, so it figures that my muscles would be naturally talented at getting SWOLE.

See, one day I was bored and decided to see how many "shups" I could do in a minute (shups are what I call push-ups). Not to brag, but it was close to a THOUSAND.

Maybe even two thousand, I don't know.

Anyways, after the shups, I did like an infinity amount of "sups" (sit-ups, duh) and then I went to bed. When I woke up the next morning, I had a beach body that would make THOR jealous!

Seriously, my washboard abs have MINI-abs of their own! And those mini-abs have mini-MINI abs that have mini-mini-MINI abs! It's just abs on abs on abs all the way down!

Now for the best part - for a small subscription fee of $9.95 twice a day, you too can get as BEEFED as me! I'll be your personal trainer, your life coach, AND your best friend for around only 800 pennies an hour!

And if you act now, you'll also get–

So, like I was saying, if you act now, you'll also get–

Grrr! IF YOU ACT NOW, YOU'LL ALSO GET–

'Kay, whatever, never mind.

# EPISODE TWO:
# SNEAKY STUNTS

For those of you just tuning in, let me give you the lowdown about who I am! The name's Davy Spencer, and it's my DESTINY to become a mega-famous YouTuber someday.

I'm not quite there yet, so you've still got time to hop onto the Davy train before it takes off – that way, you can say you were my fan BEFORE it was cool!

I mean, that won't get you any prizes or anything, but it still gives you street cred, AKA, bragging rights.

Which is also worth nothing.

Anyways, I KNOW it's my destiny, but the dumb thing about destiny is that she works on her own schedule. I'm doing everything I can to speed things up, but nothing seems to be working.

I mean, this is the SIXTH SEASON of Kid YouTuber, and I don't even have a PUBLISHING deal yet!

But THIS season is the BIG one, I can feel it! THIS is the season where everybody in the world learns who Davy Spencer is because I'm about to take it up a notch.

Actually, back up. I'm not taking it up by ONE notch. I'm taking it up by a BAJILLION notches. Look, I've learned a lot from seasons 1-5, and I'm ready to take bigger risks to achieve the Herculean level of success that's waiting for me on the other side.

Yes, that was me standing on the edge of the stairs on the second floor of Wood Intermediate. And yes, I was rockin' my brand new Sneakys that I bought over the weekend.

*Sidenote - Sneakys are a sneaker with a hidden wheel in the sole. They're basically secret roller-skates that are absolutely savage that everybody should go out and buy.

#NotSponsored

#Yet

#ButCallMeToWorkSomethingOut

And, in case it wasn't obvious enough, I was about to use my Sneakys to shred some gnarly tricks down those stairs.

Some of you probably think that's a dumb idea, and you're not wrong. During any other NORMAL week, it WOULD'VE been a dumb idea, but this isn't a normal week!

Nope, this week is Mr. Mitchell's 25th anniversary of working at the school! He's my science teacher who hates anything and everything that's fun. There's gonna be a small party in the cafeteria during lunch on Friday to celebrate, but if you ask me, that just isn't enough.

Mr. Mitchell is a fantastic teacher, but seriously? That dude's gotta lighten up a bit! He's old school – the kind of guy who thinks kids should be SEEN and not HEARD.

Anyways, I was about to launch myself into superstardom when I suddenly remembered that I had to keep an eye out for Fergus and Dutch. Those two have been killing it as hall monitors ever since the whole MISSING CHICKEN incident a few weeks back.

Fergus already told me that he wasn't gonna play favorites with anybody in the school, which basically meant that he'd bust whoever needed busting, including ME.

That's fine. I respect that.

That just meant I'd need to be a little sneakier with any wrongdoings... not that I was partaking in any wrongdoings.

After making sure the coast was clear, I went over the details one last time with my stunt coordinators just to make sure we were all on the same page.

The most important part was the ending at the bottom of the steps. That's where I told Emma Walsh to wait because I wanted to show her something super cool. When she sees me stick the landing, she'll fall head over heels in like with me because NOBODY can resist an athlete at the top of their game.

BTW, I KINDA have a thing for Emma.

The stage was set, and I was ready to rock. The only thing left to do was to actually go through with it. I grabbed the handrail and slowly rolled forward on my heels. Then I stared into the abyss for a few seconds...

I couldn't think about it anymore. Thinking about it made it scary, so I gripped the handrail, took a deep breath, and hurled myself towards my destiny.

And guess what?

I totally KILLED it because of course I did!

I nailed every sick trick on my list, even tossing in a few random tricks to add more flavor to the pot. I zigged. I zagged. I flipped. I spun. And when I landed perfectly at the bottom, everybody went BANOODLES!

For real, locker doors were blown off their hinges as kids exploded with cheers! They chanted my name, called me their hero, and all the girlies swooned over me.

Okay... fine.

My stunt wasn't as successful as I would've liked.

Instead of the dangerous feat I had spent all weekend planning (including all my allowance on for the Sneakys), I flopped down the stairs like a cold, wet hot dog. The WHOLE entire thing was an EPIC fail.

Actually, that's not true.

The ONLY part that went according to plan was that Emma waited for me at the bottom of the stairs.

TBH, I could've done without that, too.

Ugh.

As I stared up at Emma, I knew that my brain was in the middle of forming a cringe-memory - the kind of memory that lurks by your bed like a dark shadow, ready to take you down a notch by reminding you of some humiliating thing you said or did in the past.

Actually, my sister acts like that dark shadow sometimes...

And to make matters WORSE, not only did I BIFF in front of Emma, but I BIFFED right on top of some NEW KID who was just trying to find his locker! Apparently, it was LITERALLY his FIRST day at Wood, and I gave him a warm welcome by body slamming him into the floor.

I was pretty lucky that Gabe wasn't angry. Most kids would've been angry. So, I helped him up and explained what I was trying to do with my YouTube channel, but then he stopped me...

Turns out, Gabe LOVES YouTube (because who doesn't?) and that prank videos were his favorite. And I gotta say that I agree! Prank videos are the best!

I've even given some serious thought to making prank videos myself. I've got a million great ideas for pranks. In fact, I was getting goosies just thinking about them, and that's when I accidentally said my best idea out loud...

Gabe talked forever about his favorite prank videos, even busting out his phone to show me and Emma the actual videos themselves, which was a little rude because I thought we were talking about MY YouTube channel, but whatever.

And I think we all know how hard it is to watch a video that somebody else wants you to watch, right? I mean, seriously, one is bad enough, but Gabe made us watch FIVE!

Well, he made ME watch five. Emma bailed after the third one. And she didn't even use a good excuse!

And then, when the last video ended, Gabe perked up.

To be fair, it wasn't the worst request I'd ever gotten. THAT award goes to FluffyCookie_72 for saying I should invent a new drink made from mixing guacamole and milk and then calling it GuacaMilk.

Nope. Just... nope.

And for the record, no matter what Chuck tells you, I'M the one who thought GuacaMilk was a bad idea. Not him.

Anyways, pranks are a delicate artform. Prank too hard and you're a jerk. Prank too soft and what's the point? The BEST pranks are perfectly balanced between love and hate, and Gabe's snowball to the face leaned more towards hate.

Not to mention the fact that it involved resources I didn't have...

And right there, my time with Gabe came to an end because of how he said, "WE'LL figure it out." I mean, I JUST met the kid, and he was already getting clingy?

That's never a good sign.

Okay, look, I'm sure Gabe was a cool kid, but he could be cool somewhere else, you know what I mean? Besides, I was gonna be so busy making TONS of dope Sneakys videos that he would've just felt ignored. And THAT would've been unfair to HIM, so I was actually doing Gabe a favor by snubbing him, right? Right, you get it.

So, I walked away from Gabe and that was that. Or at least, I THOUGHT that was that...

# EPISODE THREE:
# BOWLING IS RIGHT UP MY ALLEY

Since my first AWESOME stunt was a bust, I went straight onto the next one because of the famous saying, "If at first you don't succeed, quit and try something else." Great advice. Paul Bunyan said that, and he was a movie star or something, so I'm pretty sure he knows a thing or two about making it big in the biz.

Let me set the scene for you - it was lunch, and it was just me, Annie, and Chuck. Fergus and Dutch were still out monitoring the halls.

My second stunt was more theatrical than the first. It involved me wearing a bowling ball helmet, and then blazing through the cafeteria in my Sneakys until I crashed into Annie and Chuck who were dressed like bowling pins!

Well, CHUCK was dressed like a bowling pin. ANNIE had to dress in her own thing because of course she did.

As soon as the bowling pin and penguin were in place, I strapped my helmet on, raised my hands over my head, and made the announcement...

When everybody's eyes were on me, I started running as fast as I could, then I leaned back on my heels and sailed across the floor like a gazelle.

But as much as I'd love to tell you that I nailed the stunt... I can't. Because right before the explosive finale, Gabe popped up outta freakin' nowhere.

I'm happy to report that on a scale of 1-10, the damage to school property was zero. However, on a scale of 1-10, the damage to my dignity was at a record high of 11.

Oh well. Gabe didn't know what I was doing, so it wasn't like he was TRYING to bomb my second stunt. Besides, it was possible that he had saved me from getting busted by Fergus and Dutch who just happened to walk into the cafeteria at that exact same time.

Welp, that was now TWO videos I had to scrap because of a failed stunt. No big deal though because I'm a pretty laidback kind of guy.

Well, that and my tummy was rumblin' for some food.

I also figured I could use what little time I had left at lunch to do a quickie food review. If I could still get ONE video done, then I wouldn't feel like my morning had been a COMPLETE waste of time.

So, me and my friends grabbed some food and found a quiet spot near the back of the cafeteria where I could film without a ton of distractions.

Too bad when you're an almost-famous YouTuber like me, distractions follow you wherever you go...

Somehow, I doubted it was a "quinky-dink."

Gabe sat with us and it was fine. I mean, it would've been MORE fine if he had talked to the rest of the gang, but he was TOTALLY snubbing them just to talk to me.

Can you blame him, though?

People get weird when they're in the presence of greatness. They get all awkward and overthink what they say, which was probably why Gabe was being so weird.

He was just in awe of a soon-to-be-famous star, and his nerves were showing, simple as that. But for real though? He was starting to overdo it with video suggestions for my channel.

I've tried the whole "food fight" thing before, but it never takes off. I've actually tried a few other times, too, but got the EXACT same results, so I know it's not ME. For some reason, kids just don't want to have a food fight.

Don't believe me? Watch...

Personally, I think kids are just scared of getting detention. I don't know how to change that, though. Being part of a full-on food fight at school has slowly become the number one item on my bucket list because I know it won't happen, never in a million, billion years.

Anyways, Gabe just kept rattling off suggestions, one after another, and it wouldn't have been so bad if he wasn't stuck on one idea the whole time...

It was starting to get annoying. But I felt bad for him because he was CLEARLY just trying to make new friends at a new school, and that's NEVER easy.

I was the new kid at the beginning of the year, so I can tell you from personal experience – it's not the best time ever.

I tried to be patient, I seriously did, but after Gabe's one millionth snowball idea, I realized I was running outta time to film my food review! Lunch was almost over, and I needed to start recording ASAP as possible!

So, I came up with a pretty clever way to make Gabe stop with his snowball ideas. See, I thought I could CANCEL OUT his prank ideas altogether... with an ANTI-prank idea.

Gabe wasn't into it.

Honestly? I have no idea WHY I thought that would work, I just thought it would... but it didn't. So, I went all old-school on him and just told him straight-up to leave.

But NICELY, obvi.

And just like that, Gabe disappeared from my life just as quickly as he came.

## EPISODE FOUR:
# LUNCH REVIEW: CHICKEN FINGERS

We all know evil scientists use middle school cafeterias as a place to destroy the evidence of their failed biological experimentations, but we've never seen proof...

Until now.

I'm Davy Spencer, and I've gone super-duper deep undercover as a regular student at Wood Intermediate to bring you the horrifying truth that is...

Chicken fingers. What exactly are they? Let's get a simple fact out of the way first... CHICKENS DON'T HAVE FINGERS.

Last time I checked, chickens don't even have arms!

Don't believe me? Have you ever LOOKED at a chicken? They got WINGS, not ARMS. Can you imagine if they HAD arms? I've asked local artist, Annie Wu, to illustrate the difference between a chicken with no arms and a chicken with arms.

It's UNNATURAL. AGAINST the laws of nature. An ABOMINATION of the natural order of things. And it's just freakin' weird! But do evil scientists care? I've asked local scientist Mr. Mitchell, what HE thought, but he DECLINED to comment.

That's exactly what EVIL scientists WANT you to think because they do whatever they want, slicing and dicing all kinds of DNA, and then fusing them together to make mutant creatures so they can sell them for STACKS of cash to alien zoos on other planets!

There's plenty of evidence of them doing this in the past. Where do you think GIRAFFES came from? Just take zebra DNA, fuse it with flamingo DNA, add a little yellow color, and BAM, you got yourself a BABY GIRAFFE. And don't even get me started on the duckbilled platypus!

You see, evil scientists are so preoccupied with whether or not they could, they don't stop to think if they SHOULD.

Which is what brings me back to the chicken fingers. Not ALL DNA fusing is a success. In fact, how much you wanna bet MOST of their experiments end in total, catastrophic failure?

So, the question you need to ask yourself is... what happens to all their FAILED experiments?

These evil scientists probably got an order from Gorgon-5 to make a PLETHORA of chickens with arms and fingers, and then at the last minute, the Gorgonian-5's CANCELED the order, leaving the Earth with a whole buttload of mutant poultry that needed to be "disappeared."

Sounds fake, I know. But don't take my word for it. Take this anonymous student's word for it...

And now, the moment you've all been waiting for - I am going to attempt to EAT a chicken's finger.

There it is! Definitive PROOF that chicken fingers are ACTUAL chicken FINGERS. See? Wedding rings are designed to be worn ONLY on fingers! So, why else would that RING have been in my food?

Annnd THAT'S where my lunch review ended. I wasn't sure what the heck happened. One second, I was talking to the camera... the next, I was sitting there with cold snow dripping off my chin, like WHAAAT?

Even my friends were confused!

None of us had a clue where that thing came from!

For a second, I thought maybe a snowball had manifested itself in the cafeteria in some kind of spontaneous act of creation in the universe, because HOW AWESOME would that have been?

But I'm sad to say that's NOT what happened.

How do I know?

Because, like, five seconds after that, the kid who threw the snowball popped up outta nowhere.

## EPISODE FIVE:
# I SPENT HALF THE DAY IN MY LOCKER

121 VIEWS 517 FANS

Sure, I might've gotten spanked in the face by a snowball, but it was just out of Gabe's love for the game!

He started his own YouTube channel because OF COURSE he did! I was the one who suggested it, so how can I be mad that he took my absolutely amazing advice?

If more people did that, then the world would be a better place.

In fact, I guarantee it!

That's why I'm letting you know, for a limited time only, I'm offering business advice to anybody who needs me to kick them in the butt and tell them what to do!

For only $250, I'll be your guiding light, and together, we'll march forward into this crazy thing called "life," and we'll OBLITERATE every obstacle that's keeping you from becoming YOU.

Annie thought I should prank Gabe back, but I didn't love that idea. If I pranked him back, then he'd prank me back-back, and I'd prank him back-back-back, and it would be this endless cycle of pranks that went on forever until we both died of old age.

Besides, Gabe already got me once.

He wasn't gonna get me a SECOND time.

So, I was free to do my next stunt, which was gonna be locking myself inside my locker for the last half of the school day!

I flipped my locker open and started pulling out all the junk that was inside. Surprisingly, it was a TON of junk. I was actually a little embarrassed about the whole thing. I mean, there was stuff in there that I didn't even remember bringing to school!

When the locker was clean, I put my foot in first, then wriggled the rest of my body in, everything except my head because... well... because my head, you see...

How can I put this... its, um... it's...

I just haven't grown into my head yet! Once I hit my teenage years, it'll all balance out. And obviously my head is so big to accommodate my bigger than average brain! And you know what they say – bigger brains means bigger smarts!

I couldn't waste any more time disputing head sizes with Annie because class was about to start. If I angled my dome just right, I could feel it start to squeeze in, but no matter how hard I pushed, it just wouldn't go! So, I stepped back to reassess the sitch… but that's when this happened…

Before I hit the ground, tiny little ice particles found their way into my mouth and up my nose and into my ears and all over my hair. My cheeks burned from getting licked in the face with a freshly rolled snowball.

My body slapped the floor like a piece of raw turkey bacon.

I was dizzy, my vision blurry as the blob of Annie knelt by my side. I think she was asking me if I was hurt, but I wasn't sure – her voice was muffled behind the high-pitched squeal coming from the depths of my ears.

In the haze behind Annie, I saw the fuzzy image of a child jogging toward us. Closer and closer he came until, at last, he slowed to a stop in front of me. I reached my hand out to the child, but he had no interest in giving aid.

Instead, he just wanted to do this...

## EPISODE SIX:
# LET'S. GET. DANGEROUS.

113 VIEWS 503 FANS

So, that was TWICE now that Gabe SNAPPED me. It was a good one, too! Came outta nowhere! Annie again suggested that I prank him back, but I was, like, "Nahhh, I'm good."

And Gabe really hit me HARD with that snowball! Like, SUPER hard. Not only in my eye, but my EAR, too! The lobe was throbbing a little and I kinda lost my hearing for a bit, but it came back during the middle of 7th period, so it's all good!

And just in time, too, because my next stunt was gonna take place as soon as school dismissed. It was gonna be a DOOZY, probably one of the most insane stunts ever done by any 10-year-old ever. It HAD to be because my first two stunts BOMBED so hard that I needed to make up for it, big time!

It was so dangerous that I even printed out a waiver for me to sign saying I wouldn't sue myself in case something went horribly wrong, and I had to go to the hospital.

Exactly thirty seconds before the last bell rang, I stood on my chair and loudly proclaimed...

Okay, I know what you're thinking. You're thinking I must be some kind of crazy person for wanting to roll across the top of a school bus, but I assure you, I'm not! Because here's my secret – the stunt SOUNDS more dangerous than it actually is!

The bus won't be moving and all I'm doing is gliding across the top of it from one end to the other. I did the math, and according to my calculations, I'm going to be just fine.

News of my amazingness spread pretty fast, and as soon as the bell rang, I already had a giant crowd following me as I led the way out of the side doors of the school, to where the buses and bike racks were. They wanted a show, and I was gonna give it to them.

But when I got to the buses, the whole thing came SCREECHING to a halt when I suddenly saw...

I was outraged! OUTRAGED, I say!

Hall Monitors only have jurisdiction INSIDE the school, which meant Fergus and Dutch couldn't tell me what to do OUTSIDE! They were clearly out of line!

GOSH, I can't even! I. LITERALLY. CAN'T. EVEN.

I bet those two even told Principal Hawkins what I was doing, too! Ugh, can you believe they'd do that??

Okay, you got me. The whole riding on top of the bus thing was just one big fake out – a PRANK, if you will. I was never gonna do it because DUH! It's dumb and dangerous and I'd like to die when I'm old and rich instead of when I'm young and broke, thank you very much.

Fergus was also in on the prank, but he was only cool with it because it meant he would just PRETEND bust me instead of for-real bust me.

Nobody got hurt and everybody got fooled! You see? THAT'S how you do it. Pranking doesn't need to be painful or anything. As long as everybody's having fun, then it's–

Okay. That was THREE times now.

THREE different times I got DOMED by a snowball.

A SNOWBALL!

DURING school!

On a HOT day!!

WHERE'S HE EVEN GETTING SNOW??

That was it – the last straw that opened the can of worms that broke the camel's legs or whatever. I was willing to ignore the first two snowballs, but NOT the third one.

Gabe was the one who started it, but I was gonna be the one to finish it...

## EPISODE SEVEN:
# BONE APPLE TEA

Gabe's gonna regret the day he decided to mess with me, which LITERALLY was yesterday. I'm gonna prank him back so hard that he won't even know what HIT him!

He'll just stand there, shocked, and I'll run in and be like...

Focusing on Gabe also means I'm switching gears. Instead of honoring Mr. Mitchell with STUNT videos, I'll honor him with PRANK videos. It's different content, but with the same big ups as before.

After school yesterday, I went home and came up with a bunch of pranks of my own. I went with a more "grown-up" approach than Gabe did, which means I didn't want to do anything that would hurt him like he did with me by THROWING A FREAKING ROCK-HARD SNOWBALL AT MY FACE.

Nope. Harmful pranks could land me in detention, so I decided to go with FOOD pranks instead.

The ingredients for crafting the perfect food prank includes patience, skill, and creativity. It also includes ACTUAL ingredients, which luckily, my parents had in their pantry.

And after a night of hard work, I had a nice bag of tricks ready to go...

That looks like a lot of pranks, I know, but I wasn't gonna serve them up at the same time. I was gonna stretch it out a little. Make it last all day, y'know?

When I got to school on Tuesday morning, I was pretty sure Gabe was gonna get me with another snowball because he's done it three times already, why not four?

So, I rushed to my locker, but as soon as I opened it, I found out I was already too late.

Gabe got me again. But not with a snowball. With sand.

Yellow sand poured out of my locker as soon as I opened it.

After that, Gabe spun around and tried to take off, but that lamewad's backpack slipped off of his shoulder and fell on the floor. Some small tubs of frosting tumbled out, which wasn't weird until he snatched them up like a hobo who just won money throwin' dice down by the train tracks.

Gabe was already gone by the time Fergus and Dutch showed up to help me clean up the sand. Part of being a Hall Monitor meant cleaning up messes in the hallways.

I asked Fergus if he was gonna bust Gabe for the prank, but he said there wasn't any evidence to PROVE it was Gabe who actually put the sand in my locker.

After ALL my careful planning, I had to wait until AFTER first period to finally get started! And to top it off, I didn't even have time to store my OTHER food pranks in my locker, so I had to lug them around in my backpack!

My first food prank was the mayo-donut. You see, it's BRILLIANT because the mayonnaise is INSIDE the donut, so Gabe won't even know what happened until AFTER he takes a bite!

My only problem was that anything delivered by ME was gonna be too obvious, so my solution to that was wearing a disguise provided by the KING of disguises, Chuck.

He's got a MILLION costumes at home.

I'm not sure why, but whatever, that's none of my business.

The costume had to be subtle. Something INCONSPICUOUS to fool even the sharpest eye because how much you wanna bet Gabe was on high alert for any pranks comin' his way? If ANYTHING was off then the prank would've flopped.

So, when Chuck showed up with the WRONG costume, I was pretty peeved! He bought me a TURTLE costume.

But not just ANY turtle...

HOW IS DRESSING LIKE LEONARDO SUPPOSED TO HELP? THAT'S THE **OPPOSITE** OF INCONSPICUOUS!
YOU NEVER SAID **DON'T** BRING LEONARDO!
IF I GOTTA TELL YOU WHAT **NOT** TO BRING, WE'D BE HERE ALL DAY!
SO, WHO DO YOU WANT?? **RAPHAEL**??
NO, DUDE! ARE YOU **FOR REAL** RIGHT NOW??
MICHELANGELO THEN??
**YES,** MICHELANGELO!

OKAY THEN! I'M SORRY FOR YELLING AT YOU! I'M JUST A LITTLE STRESSED OUT!
IT'S FINE! I UNDERSTAND, AND I FORGIVE YOU!
BROS FOREVER!
BROS FOREVER!
WAIT, WHAT JUST HAPPENED?

All that work and I had to bail on the Ninja Turtle costume because there wasn't enough time for Chuck to run home and swap costumes.

But I wasn't one to give up so fast (at least THAT time), so I quickly recruited Dutch to be my donut delivery guy.

Gabe didn't know Dutch was one of my besties, which made Dutch the perfect undercover agent for me.

Dutch was cool with it. In fact, he even knew which class Gabe had next because I guess it's his job to know? I dunno, that doesn't sound right, but whatever – the point is Dutch took me to the right spot.

I ran down the hall and peeked around the corner. Gabe was already coming our way! In just a few of seconds, he was gonna walk past Dutch who would offer him a delectable donut he won't be able to resist, and then I SHALL BE THE ONE WHO TASTES SWEET VICTORY ON THIS DAY, my friends!

So, I ran back to Dutch as fast as I could to tell him to get ready. But that's when I realized trusting Dutch with any kind of food was a bad idea...

Not only did Dutch scarf down my mayo-donut, but he scarfed down the REST of the pranks in my backpack, too! The toothpaste Oreos! The caramel onion! Even the cheese juice! ALL digesting LOUDLY in the pit of Dutch's tummy!

I was about to go Super Saiyan on him, but then he gave me the biggest puppy dog eyes I'd ever seen on a kid...

Man, who was I kidding? Only a truly heartless person could stay mad at that.

# EPISODE EIGHT:
# SNAKE IT TILL YOU MAKE IT

Yup. GABE.

When I got there, he was already in the gymnasium talking to a bunch of other kids, probably about me, I don't know. I mean, none of them looked at me, so maybe they weren't... but they probably were.

Fergus had gym, too, so I went and stood by him as we waited for Miss Gymalski to start class.

FYI - Miss Gymalski is an ex-Olympic weightlifter from Austria with a really cool Austrian accent.

I'm not sure why she teaches gym because she could easily be doing cooler things, like wrestling bears or something because she's built like a tank.

I'd even say that she's probably the strongest person in town. Nobody really knows HOW strong exactly, but there are rumors...

Anyways, I kept an eye on Gabe while I waited for gym to start. There was no way he'd prank me in the MIDDLE of a class, right? Nobody's THAT crazy. I mean, that's just ASKING for detention, isn't it?

And he didn't look over at me one single time, either, almost like he was purposely NOT looking, which TOTALLY meant he was OBVIOUSLY plotting something sinister!

Finally, Miss Gymalski marched out of the girl's locker room with sunglasses perched on her head, a stopwatch in one hand, a clipboard in the other, and a whistle hanging out of her mouth.

Those fashionably sporty accessories could only mean one thing...

Ugh. I hate running the mile. It's so pointless. So unnecessary. So HARD. My legs cramp, my side cramps, my back cramps - EVERYTHING cramps when I'm forced to run ONE MILE.

WHY'S that even a subject in school??

Like, I get why they teach math. I might not AGREE with why they teach math, but I get it.

But running a mile?

When am I ever gonna NEED to do that when I grow up?

And as everybody straggled out to the track, I suddenly remembered that I had a secret that would make me DOMINATE the mile without even breaking a sweat.

I was wearing my Sneakys.

#StillNotSponsored

#CallMeAlready

Oh, man, it was perfect!

While all the other peasants were gonna use their MUSCLES to run, I was gonna use the hidden wheels in my shoes to SAIL across the finish line. I'd probably even break the world record for fastest mile run by a 6th grader.

My life would change.

I'd be all over the news.

Get my picture in the paper.

Product endorsements.

Clothing sponsorships.

Face on the Wheaties box.

You know... little things like that, but it all adds up.

When all the students were on the track, we bunched up at the starting line as Miss Gymalski stood in front of us holding the stopwatch over her head.

I pushed myself through the crowd to get to the front. That way I wouldn't have to worry about passing other kids as I secretly skated my way to victory.

Beating everybody out there was gonna be cake - everybody except for one person - Fergus. He was the only one I had to worry about because he had a special racing wheelchair.

I mean, the thing looked like a freakin' racecar!

How was that even fair to everybody else??

Gabe was right behind me, which was great because I wanted him to eat my dust the most. I think I had him pretty nervous because he knelt down to tie his shoes tighter.

Was he gonna try to race me?

LOL.

Can you believe that??

Gabe had no idea how badly he was about to get schooled.

I actually would've felt sorry for the kid if he wasn't annoyingly nudging my feet the whole time, but whatever. I ignored it since Miss Gymalski had already started the countdown.

I had to focus. Eyes on the prize. Stay positive. Work hard. Make it happen. Dance like nobody's watching.

Wait, no, that last one is... never mind, it works.

Miss Gymalski was down the last three seconds, but before she could finish, everybody around me suddenly freaked out. I wasn't sure what was going on until Gabe shouted...

That thing was bright red and yellow and vicious looking!

It was also RIGHT BEHIND my shoe!

I started running as the other kids scattered, and out of the thirty students out there, guess who the deadly snake decided to chase?

I ran faster than I'd ever run before in my entire life, but no matter how fast I went, the snake perfectly kept up.

And NOBODY helped me out, not even Miss Gymalski! Nope, everybody was having a good ol' time on the sidelines watching the last few seconds of my life before that killer snake caught me and sucked all the blood from my body!

*DAVY'S NOTE: IT WAS VAMPIRES.

I was on my own, which was fine by me. I didn't need their help anyway! I control my own fate, and I wasn't about to let some snake defeat me in front of my classmates!

I dove onto the grass and started rolling around like I was on fire, hoping to scare the snake away, but it didn't work. The slithery reptile bounced around me the whole time like it was made out of rubber!

Suddenly, it jumped straight for my face probably because it wanted to bite it off, but right before it got me, I grabbed its squishy body with both of my hands.

But the fight wasn't over.

Not by a long shot.

In front of all my peers, I wrestled that snake like a BOSS. I just needed to wear the sucker out so it wouldn't fight me anymore, and it was working! The snake wasn't putting up much of a fight in my hands!

Actually, it wasn't fighting at all. Like, not even a little. That's when I stopped to look at the snake's weird, spongy face, and then I realized...

The fake snake had a string tied around its neck. The other end of that string... was attached to my shoe.

Gabe wasn't nudging my feet earlier. He was setting me up for another prank! I expected Miss Gymalski to do the right thing and send that kid to detention, but guess what?

She DIDN'T. Because as it turns out... she's a huge fan of Gabe's YouTube channel.

# EPISODE NINE:
# VIEWER REQUEST: MOON LANDING

One of my awesome Fans asked me to build a rocketship to fly to the moon, which... isn't exactly EASY.

But it's also not IMPOSSIBLE, not when you're a creative genius like me!

Obviously, I can't build a REAL rocketship and fly it around in outer space because of intergalactic space laws and stuff, so I'm just gonna have to do the next best thing...

I'm just gonna have to fake it.

See, Fergus' parents just got him some high-end CGI software that he's been itching to use. It's the same software Hollywood uses for their movies, so it's legit.

You wanna see a gigundo explosion go off behind me and my squad while we walk away in super-duper slow-motion?

Not even a problem...

But a CGI trip to the moon wasn't enough for me, no way. I wanted to take the viewer request above and beyond by turning it into a mini movie!

And while me, Annie, Chuck, and Fergus spent a few hours making cardboard backdrops, Dutch spent that whole time writing up a script.

And finally, ladies and gentlemen, without further ado, I proudly present to you...

Captain's log, stardate 0.7734.

This is Captain Davy Spencer reporting in.

It has only been one week since Mission Control received a mysterious S.O.S. signal from the moon, but it feels like forever ago.

Me and my crewmates, Commander Annie Wu and Lieutenant Commander Dutch McKenzie, have been training non-stop and extra hard for the super-duper-ultra-mega-top-secret mission of investigating the source of the S.O.S.

Major Fergus Widdershim maintains that it WASN'T a trap set by alien monsters who want to eat us when we get there, but I strongly disagree.

One of us will be wrong about that.

I think it's him, but I hope it's me.

Annie, Dutch, and I had just buckled our seatbelts in the hottest new spaceship this side of the galaxy, the Best Friends Forever 5, or the BFF5 for short.

Major Fergus hopped on the intercom and started the countdown...

Not sure why he started at such a high number, but whatevs. That extra time just gave me and my crewmates some time to bond.

That took me by surprise. Me and Annie had been training with Dutch 24/7 in the last week, but that was the first time he ever mentioned being married with a kid!

Turns out, because of our intense training, Dutch had to miss the birth of his first child, Otto. Dutch knew that would happen when he signed up.

You see, before he volunteered for the moon mission, Dutch was serving a life sentence for stealing bread... to feed the homeless?

And this mission was his "get out of jail free" card and he couldn't wait to get home to hold his newborn baby??

Okay, come on...

Fergus finally got to zero and the BFF5's rockets flared up.

We had liftoff.

Me, Annie, and Dutch got jolted back. Our ship climbed higher and higher, faster and faster. That kind of speed really takes its toll on the human body, especially in the FACIAL regions of the human body.

As soon as we broke atmo, our ship switched from the normal engines over to the FTL (Faster Than Light) drive, which was an experimental new engine that had never even been TESTED before because it had only been invented 24 hours ago by some computer hackers in Europe.

It takes NASA three days to fly to the moon, but with the FTL engine, we could do it in less than a minute. At least, that's what was SUPPOSED to happen if everything had gone according to plan.

I clicked the button to initiate the FTL drive, but it needed about 30 seconds to warm up. The BFF5 shook as the FTL drive hummed to life.

That's when Fergus' voice broke over our headsets.

The three of us looked out the front window. There, in the vast emptiness of outer space, we saw a basketball-sized meteor gunning toward us, leaving a trail of fire and ice behind it.

I grabbed the steering wheel, cranked it hard to the left, and hit the gas. The BFF5 spun around, but it was too late...

The crew was fine. I wish I could say the same for the FTL drive. The stray meteor had punched that thing square in the face, completely turning our ship around, which gave us a much WORSE problem to deal with – the FTL drive was still firing up, but instead of facing the moon, it was facing the Earth. In about 20 seconds, the BFF5 would shoot directly into the planet faster than the speed of light.

Nobody knows what a collision of that magnitude would do to our planet, but probably not good things – duh.

In other words, A TON of people were about to kick the bucket.

Everybody in the cockpit went silent. We looked at each other knowing full well that whoever went outside to fix that drive... was doomed.

And by DOOMED, I mean DEAD.

And by DEAD, I mean, like, SUPER DEAD. Like, NEVER-GOING-BACK-HOME-DEAD because they'll be a floating popsicle in outer space for, like, forever.

Nobody wanted to go, but one of us HAD to. And as captain of the BFF5, it was gonna be me, obvi.

I unbuckled my seatbelt and started floating to the backdoor. I made a quick stop at the bathroom to double check if I was wearing clean undies.

Grandma always said, "Make sure you're wearing clean underwear just in case you have to sacrifice yourself realigning an FTL drive in outer space someday!"

I never understood what she meant by that until now.

After my bathroom break, I continued floating to the backdoor. When I got there, I reached for the handle, but I stopped suddenly.

Resting on top of the handle... was a baby rattle.

That's when I looked up through the window on the door...

What the heck was Dutch doing??

As the captain of the ship, it was MY job to save the crew!

But no matter how much I yelled at Dutch, he wouldn't listen! He just kept making his way to the messed up FTL drive. I tried to reason with him. There was still time for us to swap spots!

But he ignored me.

The ship suddenly started shaking.

The FTL drive was firing up.

Only a few more seconds until it popped.

Dutch made it to the drive and realigned it without a problem. I hoped he could make it back to the door before we took off, but...

There was a flash of light and the BFF5 took off faster than the speed of light.

When I looked out the window, Dutch was gone.

The BFF5 made it to the moon in less than a minute, as advertised. When we were over our landing zone, I shut off the drive, but it didn't slow us down enough.

I guess that's the problem with untested technology... whatever CAN go wrong WILL go wrong.

Our ship BOOM SHAKALA'D into the surface like a bug on a windshield.

Me and Annie were lucky to survive the crash. The SHIP was toast, but we could worry about that AFTER the mission, which was to find the source of the S.O.S. signal.

Annie said the signal was close, but I couldn't see signs of alien life anywhere.

I could, however, HEAR it.

And it DIDN'T sound friendly – like a grumbly tummy mixed with a wet burp mixed with nails on a chalkboard. But me and Annie had a job to do, so we walked toward the gross sound, only to find...

Me and Annie were about to do battle with the alien monster, but that's when our movie making came to a screeching halt by some kinda weird object hovering right above us in the sky...

Dutch and Fergus joined me, Annie, and Chuck as we stared at the thing over our heads. It had a blinking red light and was putting out a high-pitched buzzing sound.

I squinted to see it better because the sky was so dark, and suddenly, I knew what I was looking at...

UFO's are a lot smaller than I thought they'd be, but nobody knows how big REAL aliens are. Maybe they're tiny! Maybe that thing was PACKED with a dozen little alien dudes!

Oh, man, how adorbs would THAT be?? ITSY BITSY, CUTIE-PATOOTIE, aliens - ohmagoshhhhh! If I caught REAL aliens on camera, then my video would become the most watched video IN HISTORY. So, I raised my hands to let my new alien friends know I wasn't a threat!

Then the UFO lowered enough so I could see every tiny detail on the ship, and THAT'S when I realized I had made a HORRIBLE mistake.

It was DEFINITELY a flying object, but it was no longer UNIDENTIFIED.

The saucer I'd been staring at? Yeah, that wasn't the bottom of a spaceship... it was the bottom of a pie pan.

And that annoying buzzing sound? Oh, that was coming from the drone that was CARRYING the pie pan right before DROPPING it on my face.

And also – it was Gabe's drone.

I knew it was his because he had a little speaker hooked up to it so I could hear his voice...

# EPISODE TEN:
# CREEPIN' IT REAL

On Wednesday morning, I went to school ready to rock round 2 of the prank war... or was it round 3?

I don't even know anymore.

And for my first prank of the day, I planned to scare the WHAT out of him with my murder-clown mask.

Jump scares are supes basic as far as pranks go, but at that point, I didn't care as long as it worked.

All I needed was to find Gabe, put on my mask, hide around the corner, and then jump out and give him a heart attack.

But as soon as I got to school, I spotted him pretty much right off the bat and... let's just say that I got a little OVER-excited. I pulled the mask over my face, but instead of hiding around the corner like I SHOULD have... I ran out, desperately waving my arms like a crazy person shouting "RAAAWR!" as loudly as I could.

Yeah, NOBODY was scared by that.

But at least I got a new cringe-memory out of it.

With that prank out the window, I went straight onto the next one, which involved me wearing an oversized teddy bear that I brought from home. That thing was just rotting away in my basement, anyways, so I figured nobody would care if I used it. I bet nobody even realized it was gone.

So, here's the prank - after first period, I asked Annie to give Gabe a fake note from an ANONYMOUS Fan saying there was a gift waiting for him in the lobby.

Gabe is such a sucker that he'll think the fan mail is legit. Then, when he sees the teddy bear, he'll be like, "Aw, cool, a teddy bear!"

After that he'll try to pick it up, and THAT'S when I'll jump up and scare him, like BOOYAH!

Annie was already on her way with the fake note, so all I had to do was get into the teddy bear, which ended up being a little harder than I thought. I mean, my body fit just fine, but there was another part of me that had a little trouble with it...

Anyways, after I made it work, I sat in the lobby and waited for Gabe to show up. Annie was supposed to deliver the fake fan mail right at the beginning of our break between classes, so Gabe was gonna come by at any second...

That wad sure took his sweet time coming to the lobby, long enough that it got hard for me to keep my eyes open.

I mean, it was just so warm and floofy inside that oversized teddy bear, is anybody even surprised that THIS happened??

Soooo, yeah, I woke up during the middle of second period when my name got called over the intercom to report to the front office.

I got up, groggy and confused from my short nap, and shuffled down the hallway until I got to the front office where everybody just stared at me all wide-eyed.

Because I totally forgot I was still wearing the teddy bear.

Then the lady behind the front desk called for Principal Hawkins to come out.

I frantically tried taking the suit off, but that didn't go so well either. The body came off easily, but the head wouldn't budge. No matter how hard I twisted, it just wasn't moving!

I was stuck!

And as if THAT wasn't bad enough, I was about to get chewed out by Hawkins for SKIPPING CLASS! Alright, look, I've gotten in trouble for all kinds of things at school, but SKIPPING CLASS has never been one of them!

I had no idea what to expect! Detention? Suspension? Expulsion? ALL of the above??

Lucky for me, it was none of those things, because as soon as Hawkins saw me, he started laughing like crazy.

Hawkins tried to pull the mask off, but he couldn't get it either. Some of the staff gave it their best shot, but nope. Then, some dude suggested getting Miss Gymalski to muscle it open, but I refused to let that She-Hulk come near me.

So, basically, I had a teddy bear head and there was literally NOTHING I could do about it!

Everybody was silent for a second.

Then, with an itty-bitty smirk, Hawkins said, "I guess you just go back to class." After that, he just WALKED BACK TO HIS OFFICE like it was NO BIG DEAL.

He thought it was FUNNY!

But what he didn't understand was that getting my head stuck in a bear head was something that was gonna follow me for the rest of my life!

I'll be the weird kid that everybody's always whispering about. And not weird like Greg Gamby. He's that kid who's always trying to start tickle fights with everybody...

I mean, yeah, that's weird, but the bear head was WEIRDER!

Kids'll make up stories like I grew up in the forest and was raised by bears, so I thought I was a REAL bear or some kind of EQUALLY deranged story like that, I don't know!

All I knew was that going back to class lookin' like that was DEFINITELY NOT A GOOD THING!

But, in the end... I didn't have a choice.

I had to get back to class.

Bear mask and everything.

Everybody laughed and pointed and blah blah blah, pretty much what you'd expect. I'm not gonna show you ALL the embarrassing moments, but I think this one scene at lunch pretty much sums up what the rest of my day was like...

Oh, and you're probably wondering what prank Gabe pulled on me during the day, too, right? It wasn't a small one, that's for sure. I'd even call it impressive if I wasn't the guy getting pranked.

It was a loud one that involved a bunch of other kids.

And it was something that made everybody look because it was impossible to ignore.

Gabe got drummers from the school marching band to follow me around lunch while playing their snare drums.

## EPISODE ELEVEN:
# VIEWER REQUEST: MALL MAGIC

He got me good three days in a row, so I'm officially throwing in the towel.

Do you hear that, Gabe? Because I know you're watching! I'm DONE. It's OVER. You win, I lose, whatever.

But it's not QUITTING! It's FORFEITING, which is totally different.

It's more honorable this way.

I'm admitting that Gabe BESTED me in a prank war that I never agreed to join. But that doesn't mean I'm gonna pout about it! No, it means I'm giving him an internet fist-bump and saying, "Good game, my dude! Now leave me alone FOREVER because I'm about to LOSE my FREAKING mind."

So, to get my mind back to normal, I decided the best thing to do was to make another viewer request, this time from a Fan who wanted me to perform magic at the mall.

First, I had to decide what kind of magic to perform.

It had to be something big and eye-catching, almost like a performance. In fact, a lot of magicians even dance before their tricks, so I had to keep that in mind, too.

Sawing someone in half is old school, but CLASSIC, one that EVERYBODY loves. I was pretty excited to try it out, and I bet it would've been BONKERS if my only volunteer hadn't chickened out about doing it.

Actually, it was hard getting ANY of the gang onboard with me - didn't even matter what the trick was. I'm not sure they even WANTED to help!

So, I had to do something on my own, which – no big deal. Tons of magicians go solo. It was probably better that way since I wouldn't have to pay anybody for being in the act.

And after some light brainstorming, I finally figured out what kind of magic I was gonna perform.

Escape acts have been around for, like, a HUNDO years, so people know what to expect when they're watching.

That's part of the fun, though, isn't it?

We've all seen the dude in the straitjacket get locked in a box, and we all know he's gonna escape, but we still can't look away because... what if he doesn't?

Wanna know the best part about a trick like that? It's 100% FAKE. That guy was NEVER in any danger! Heck, he probably wasn't even LOCKED up. All he needed to do was make the people THINK he was locked up, and BOOM – he's got everybody's attention.

With that in mind, I grabbed my dad's baggiest winter jacket along with a big ol' plastic tub from my garage and headed to the mall with my stage crew, AKA, my buds.

Setting up for the trick was cake.

All we did was go to the food court, push some tables together, and then set the plastic tub on top. As soon as that was done, I got right down to business, dancing to music that Fergus played through a Bluetooth speaker.

I know it looked silly, but I needed an audience!

Think about it – if I just dove into the plastic tub, would anyone even have noticed?

Nope.

So, I did a little dancing to spice things up! It was a marketing stunt, and it worked like a charm! Within MINUTES, I had a whole crowd of a couple people on the floor watching me!

Finally, with Chuck's help, I got into my dad's baggy jacket. Then he tied the arms behind my back, double-knotted, of course, because I couldn't make it look too easy.

With the music still playing, I shimmied over to the plastic tub, stepped inside, and let Dutch close the top, sealing me in complete darkness.

In exactly one minute, I was gonna jump out and "WOW!" my audience! Then my friends were gonna cheer loudly and get everybody to give me a standing ovation!

Oh, man, it was gonna be so wicked sweet!

But first, I needed to make it look so wicked real!

I needed to LOOK like I was struggling with trying to escape, like my life depended on it, so I started wiggling around a little.

Everybody outside was probably like, "Ohmagooooodness! Get him out before he dies! Somebody saaaaave him!"

The plan was for me to bust out after a minute, but I started feeling like that might've been way too fast for an escape act of that magnitude, so... I decided to drag it out a little.

Then, at last, I burst out of the top of the box and proclaimed my ultimate victory!

All eyes were on me as I caught my breath.

My friends were gone. Nobody cheered. Story of my life.

It was so quiet, I could hear people chewing their food! I mean, come on! That was still a great performance! Nobody was even clapping! Okay, wait, I take that back...

ONE person was clapping, but it was slow and sarcastic.

And it pretty much meant I was in deep, deep trouble...

EPISODE TWELVE:
# PINCHED

So, yeah, THAT happened.

I tried talking my way out of it, but it's hard to think when you just got caught red-handed. Pretty sure most of what came out of my mouth was jibber jabber.

I didn't really have a choice because the mall security guard, JEFF, basically dragged me back to his office.

Jeff was a pimply faced, gangly teenager wearing a uniform two sizes too big for him. He was clearly a worm who was hungry for power... but that didn't mean I wasn't scared of him.

I'd never been busted by mall security before, so I didn't know what to expect. But it couldn't be THAT bad, right?

Everybody knows that mall cops have the same amount of power as school hall monitors do. Which is basically nothing. The only difference is that mall cops are paid.

Jeff's a rent-a-cop, not a police officer.

It's not like he was gonna put me in a jail cell or something.

At least... I HOPED he wouldn't.

Jeff was mostly silent until he shut his office door. That's when he went off on me...

Okay, so things might've been a little worse than I thought.

I didn't think I was breaking the law! A little bit of horseplay at school never got me into a ton of trouble - at the worst, I got detention!

But I wasn't at school.

I was in the REAL world with REAL consequences.

My heart started racing. Sweat beaded up on my forehead. My fingers shook so bad that I put them under my legs to hide them, but that didn't matter because my legs were shaking, too!

All I wanted were my parents.

If they knew I was being held by mall security against my will, they'd scold Jeff so bad that he'd feel the burn for the rest of his life! My mom is like a ferocious mama-bear when it comes to protecting her little cubbies.

I needed to get ahold of her. I needed her to rescue me!

So, I pounded my fist on Jeff's desk and demanded that he give me the phone call that I was entitled to!

Jeff didn't even blink. He just glared at me and said...

Jeff explained (in a cheerfully villainous way) that he HAD to call the police. It's protocol whenever somebody in the mall breaks the law.

That's when the room started spinning.

My stomach turned over and over and over.

I was gonna be sick.

All I wanted to do was make a magic video! To DELIGHT others with my handsome face and a fantastic show and maybe take some donations if they liked what they saw, but what I got instead was a whole world of trouble!

And I didn't even know WHAT KIND of trouble!

I pleaded with Jeff to just let me go. I promised him that I'd never return to the mall ever, EVER again! That I'd ban MYSELF from coming back for the rest of my life if he would just let me leave before the police got there!

But Jeff wouldn't budge.

He said I deserved whatever punishment the police were gonna give me, which freaked me out even more.

That's when I went into a full-blown panic sobbing with tears and everything, but can you blame me? What started as an innocent magic trick was about to end with me GOING TO JAIL.

I think Jeff started feeling sorry for me, because that's when he tried to help by saying it probably wasn't gonna be as bad as I thought. But all that did was make it worse.

At any second, the police would storm in and take me away.

The next time I see my parents will be through a thick pane of glass.

The next time I hear their voices will be through a phone in the wall.

The next time I hug my baby sister, she'll be half a foot taller.

And the next time I see Bo-Bo, he'll be six feet under.

Finally, there was a knock at the door.

I buried my face in my trembling hands as Jeff got up to answer it. I was about to get hauled off by a police officer, and there was nothing I could do about it.

The door slowly creaked open, and I waited patiently for somebody to read me my rights, but...

That never happened. Instead, I heard this...

My mind was a mushy mess.

It took me a second to figure out what was going on.

I stared at the kid in the doorway. My eyes knew it was Gabe, but my brain wasn't so sure.

The whole thing... was a prank?

Then I remembered that Gabe said he had an older brother who got a job at the mall and that we could use him to prank people.

Jeff was Gabe's older brother!

I was NEVER in any trouble. The police were never called. Everything was going to be fine, but I was still in complete shock. Like, TRAUMATIZED shocked.

Gabe and Jeff laughed their butts off at me as I sat there in silence, dead-eyed and mouth open.

Actually, I was like that for the rest of the night...

WE'RE DONE HERE. YOU CAN LEAVE.
DID YOU HAVE A GOOD TIME AT THE MALL?
I MADE YOUR FAVE! MAC AND CHEESE WITH KETCHUP!

I'LL TAKE NINJAS FOR 2,000.
CAN WE CHANGE THE CHANNEL? THIS SHOW'S BORING.
G'NITE, DAVY! LOVE YOU!
9:30
crickets chirping
11:59

And then, at midnight, I suddenly got spanked by an idea so brilliant that Einstein himself would've given me a pat on the back.

It was for a prank to END the prank war once and for all.

After that, I slept like a baby...

## EPISODE THIRTEEN:
# IT WAS ALWAYS MINT TO BE

169 VIEWS 423 FANS

I was up bright and early and waiting outside the school at 6:30 in the morning to set up the Prank to End All Pranks

BTW, that's what I'm calling it now so get onboard.

The only downside to being at school at 6:30 a.m. was that the doors didn't open until 7:00 a.m. Oh, well, no bigs.

That gave me plenty of extra time to plan out the details of the Prank to End All Pranks...

Okay, I changed my mind – I hate that name. I'm gonna call it "The Big One" instead.

Anyways, remember that one time when I did the Diet Koala and Mintos thing in the cafeteria? If not, it's kind of a long story... this one time I did the Diet Koala and Mintos thing in the cafeteria.

Okay, so, maybe it wasn't THAT long of a story.

Everybody knows that when you drop a Mintos into a bottle of Diet Koala, the universe freaks out and makes all the suds inside go nuts and then the soda shoots out of the top like a fountain!

Sooo, that's pretty much the gist of my prank on Gabe.

I was gonna soak that dude with soda by putting Diet Koala INSIDE his locker and then set it up so that when he opens the door, a Mintos would drop into the bottle.

It was brilliant. BRILLIANT, I tell you!

And as soon as 7:00 a.m. rolled around, the doors opened, and I ran inside.

The halls were mostly empty that early in the morning. It was just me and a couple dozen randos along with the school Hall Monitors, Fergus and Dutch.

Here's where The Big One got tricky. I needed to get into Gabe's locker, but it was locked, so I needed a skeleton key (a special key that opens ALL the lockers). And there were only two places where I could find one of those – the front office and the Hall Monitor's office.

I wasn't about to try and steal the key from the front office because that'd be impossible. So, that meant I was on my way to the Hall Monitor's office.

Okay, okay, wait! STEAL is too strong of a word.

BORROW is what I meant.

I was gonna RETURN it afterward, so technically it was BORROWING.

Anyways, I figured I'd just stroll into the empty Hall Monitor office, snatch the master key, and leave, but it was a little harder than that because Fergus was inside.

Actually, never mind, it wasn't that hard.

Fergus was too busy doing paperwork to notice what I was even doing, and Dutch wasn't even there yet.

Don't you love it when things turn out to be WAY easier than you thought they'd be? I grabbed the key and ducked out, easy peasy. After that, I ran down to Gabe's locker and opened that sucker up, no problem.

The inside was pretty clean, but only because he was the new kid. Give it a month and I bet you a thousand bucks it'll look like mine. The only thing inside was a bunch of boxes of unopened cupcake mix sitting at the bottom, like, what?

Weird, right?

I mean, first, those tubs of frosting rolled out of his backpack on Tuesday, and now there's cupcake mix in his locker? I don't know, maybe he's planning a birthday party or something, whatever, I didn't care. I had a job to do.

After a few minutes, The Big One was finally set up and ready. I shut Gabe's locker door and just in the nick of time, too, because that's when he walked around the corner.

He even saw me standing there, which would've totally spoiled the whole thing if it weren't for some quick thinking.

Gabe was ALREADY suspicious that I was out to get him, so I used that to my advantage. I pulled out the leftover Mintos and offered him one with a super sneaky smile.

Success! I threw Gabe off the scent of my REAL prank by offering him a FAKE prank! Man, am I good or what??

The hallways started filling up with other students as I slowly walked down the hall, keeping an eye over my shoulder because Gabe was already spinning the combination on the lock.

In just a few seconds, he was gonna open the door, The Big One was gonna go off, and Gabe was gonna get drenched in front of EVERYBODY!

Then I was gonna roll in on my Sneakys and be like, "SORRY, NOT SORRY!" as the whole school declared me the winner of the prank war!

I'd probably even get myself a trophy for it.

Finally, Gabe finished spinning the lock. He pulled up on the handle of his locker, yanking the door wide open...

And that's when everything went wrong.

It turns out, the Mintos fell into the suds BEFORE they were supposed to. The whole time they were in Gabe's locker, the pressure was building in each bottle. And by the time he opened the door, the pressure was too much, and every bottle of Diet Koala burst at the same time.

Gabe got knocked against the wall as a storm of fizzy soda splattered everywhere. Somebody screamed, which made everybody else in the hallway panic, and that's when kids started slipping on Diet Koala.

When it was over, the hallway was filled with a dozen soggy kids laying in a puddle of Diet Koala, wondering what the heck just happened.

That's when I rolled in on my Sneakys, and said the thing, which, if I'm being honest, felt totes inappropes at the time...

So, yeah.

I got detention for the rest of the day because of that.

# EPISODE FOURTEEN: CONSEQUENCES

Gabe was the only one I wanted to prank, but it pretty much nailed everybody in that hallway. A few people got bumped and bruised, but nothing too serious.

Principal Hawkins wasn't happy about it either, obviously. And that was EVEN AFTER I told him I was only trying to HONOR Mr. Mitchell for being an awesome teacher for TWENTY-FIVE YEARS!

But then Fergus got all mad, too. Like, FOR REAL mad!

At first, I thought it was because I borrowed the skeleton key, but it wasn't that! It was because I FORCED him to bust me, but I never FORCED him to do anything! I don't even know WHY he was so angry about it, but whatever!

I guess WE'RE fighting now.

Even Dutch got on the Davy-hating bandwagon, but only because I made a huge mess in the hallway with Diet Koala.

So, I spent the rest of the day rotting away in detention, which was pretty much torture because I had to be alone in a freezing cold room with nothing else but my own thoughts.

And whenever I have that much time to sit and think about what I've done, I always come to the same conclusion...

# EPISODE FIFTEEN:
# A NEW DAY... VID

Things are going to look a bit different around here. I've had all day to ponder on it, and I've decided that it's for the best.

You see, getting detention was my wake-up call. I'm NEVER going to achieve my dreams, but I'm at peace with that. There are more important things in life, like mortgages, stock markets, and taking vitamins – which reminds me, I'll have to remember to buy some B12 later.

No, life is MORE than just goofing off and having fun. It's about becoming an adult and doing mature things like drinking coffee and watching the news, along with your cholesterol, am I right or am I right?

And to all my Fans out there, I hope you'll stick with me as my channel grows. It won't be as colorful and random as before, but I think you'll find the new format predictable yet comforting.

So, to kick things off, I decided to make a quiche with my special guest, Sir Quackingham Palace, the duck!

Quiches are a fantastic source of essential vitamins and minerals. A single slice of quiche has iron, vitamin C and protein – all necessary components for your growing body! And they're a pretty cheap meal, too, since the main ingredients are eggs!

And yes, I heard what Chuck said, but I was in the middle of making a food video, and I was pretty sure Fergus didn't actually want to talk to me, so... I ignored it.

Anyways, the first thing you'll want to do when baking a quiche is set the oven to the right temperature, which will vary depending on the type of quiche you're baking.

Is it vegetarian? Cheese? Meat-lovers? Crust? Crustless, for my gluten-free fans? Not to worry because figuring it out is easy peasy! Simply look at the directions on the box that your quiche came in!

Just pop that gorgeous pie in the oven, set the timer, and you're done. Well, at least until the timer goes off. Then you'll have to take it out and let it cool, but until then, find something productive to do - put up some drywall, go golfing, or be like me and dig into a good book!

I find that reading is a great way to become smart, don't you?

And since knowledge is power, being smart... is good.

After scanning my dad's bookshelf for a minute, I finally found a book that would help me better understand the financial climate we're living in today.

But to be honest, I couldn't understand a LICK of what that book said. I'd read a page, and then have to go back and re-read that same page because I stopped paying attention halfway through.

I kept going over the same page again and again, but none of it made any sense. Digital currency with volatile prices and blockchains and decentralized technology spread across bunches of computers, and somehow FARMING is involved, like WHAT??

I thought farmers planted crops, not coins!

That's when the timer on my quiche went off.

45 minutes had passed. 45 minutes of re-reading page 1 of the crypto book. 45 minutes of trying to be mature and my brain was ALREADY crying.

I was done with it. I have the rest of my life to be mature, but only a few more years to be a kid, so I think I should really take advantage of the little time I have left.

Well, that's not TOTALLY true.

I mean, there are gonna be situations where being mature is the way to go, and one of those situations just happened to be waiting for me right next door.

Quiche in hand, I walked over to Fergus' house and found him in his backyard with Annie and Dutch. So, I marched right up to him, and said what NEEDED to be said...

I WAS kidding.

After my dumb joke, I said what ACTUALLY needed to be said and hoped that me and Fergus would be cool again.

I knew that Fergus wouldn't forgive me right away.

That kind of thing doesn't happen in real-life.

Nobody's THAT nice.

If it were me, I know I'd need a couple days to cool off. Maybe even a couple more days after that just to prove my point.

But I didn't want it to take any longer than it needed to.

Hopefully my quiche offering was a step in the right direction. It was only Thursday night, so maybe by Saturday, we'd be cool again and could have a sleepover or something.

I mean, it WAS a four-cheese quiche, and Fergus is a HUGE fan of cheese, so that would defs help.

But then Fergus totally pulled a Fergus, and said...

Fergus forgave me ON THE SPOT because of course he did. I'm not even sure he's capable of being mad at someone for longer than an hour. I mean, that's not a BAD thing!

If everybody in the world was only HALF as nice as Fergus, then it'd be a better place, for sure.

After that, I dished out slices of quiche to my friends, which BTW, they absolutely LOVED. Pretty sure I've got a future in baking if this whole YouTuber thing doesn't work out. Well, at least baking previously FROZEN meals.

And while we chowed down, I humbly suggested watching Gabe's channel. Why? Because I knew it was gonna be packed with embarrassing prank videos of myself, but that was the point – I figured we all could use a good laugh.

So, Fergus pulled up Gabe's channel on his computer, and we watched. And laughed. And watched some more. And laughed some more.

I gotta admit that Gabe's videos weren't that bad, and I'm not talkin' about content – I'm talking about QUALITY. All were high-def with pretty kickbutt audio. I mean, you could really hear the CRUNCH of the snowballs I took to the face!

His intros weren't bad either. He had a solid background with great lighting. You could see EVERYTHING behind him, too - Lego sets, dirty laundry, books and stuff. I could even see some cupcake liners and a pack of small balloons on the desk behind him!

I'm not really sure why, but that's when I got this weird feeling in the pit of my stomach.

Like something was OFF about Gabe's video...

Like something in it was trying to get my attention...

Like my brain had figured something out before I did...

Oh, well.

Whatever, I guess. I shrugged it off and spent the rest of the night goofing off with my friends.

# EPISODE SIXTEEN:
# EMERGENCY UPLOAD

I know I should've been asleep, but I'd been up all night tossing and turning until I finally just rolled out of bed and pulled up Gabe's video on my phone to watch it again.

And that time, I saw exactly what my brain was trying to make me see earlier! I don't know what was wrong with me before – it was so obvious!

It was the cupcake liners and balloons on the desk behind him!

Okay, wait. Let me explain. By ITSELF, the liners and balloons weren't a big deal. But when they're combined with the OTHER stuff Gabe had this week, then it's a SUPER MEGA MASSIVELY BIG deal!

First, I saw the tubs of frosting roll out of Gabe's backpack! THEN I saw that cupcake mix in his locker! And now there's a pack of balloons on the desk behind him??

I mean, come on! Can't you see what he's planning?? No? Here, peep this clip from earlier this week...

That dude is gonna jack my idea after I SPECIFICALLY told him NOT to! Can you believe he'd do that?? Gah! I bet he's even the kind the of kid who would steal all your diamonds in Minecraft!

So, not only did I have the problem of intellectual property theft, but I also had the problem of getting pranked again!

And then it hit me – I suddenly knew what Gabe's next move was gonna be, which is a HUGE advantage to me, but what can I do with that information?

Do I try to prank Gabe first? No, because I don't want to make Fergus mad again.

Do I tell Fergus about the prank? If I did then Gabe might get busted, but would it teach him a lesson? Prob'ly not.

So, do I play dumb and let him just GIVE me the fake cupcake and then pop it in HIS dumb face instead of MINE?

Yes. Yes, I do.

Think about it!

Gabe'll get PLASTERED with frosting by his own prank in front of everybody! PLUS, Fergus can't be mad at me if the cupcake's FROM Gabe! I'll just act like I had no idea and be all, "Holy spaghetti and meatballs! I had no idea it would do that!"

Gabe's prank will literally blow up in his face, and I'll catch the whole thing on my camera, and at long last, I'll finally get to say what I've been wanting to say alllll week...

## EPISODE SEVENTEEN:
# THE CUPCAKE HEARD ROUND THE WORLD

I got to school around 7:35-ish, not too early, not too late, a perfectly unsuspicious time so Gabe wouldn't catch on to the fact that I totes knew what was about to go down.

Part of being "unsuspicious" also meant I couldn't wear my "BOOYAH BLING BLING!" outfit that I normally wear when I want to smear my victory in somebody else's face...

When I got to school, I waited in the lobby and tried to look as unsuspicious as possible, like some kind of gullible moron just ASKING to be pranked.

But I learned a valuable lesson that morning – trying to look UNSUSPICIOUS just makes you look MORE suspicious, which is counter-productive if you ask me.

Pretty sure that's why Gabe didn't try to get me with the fake cupcake when he showed up.

Okay, I admit that wasn't exactly SUBTLE.

Gabe cocked an eye at me as I put out the vibe, but he didn't take the bait. He just chuckled to himself and walked away WITHOUT pranking me!

That's fine.

School hadn't even started yet. There was still plenty of time to get him to fall for my trap. I tried again after first period, even using a prop I got from the band room, but Gabe was smarter than he looked. He saw right through my feeble attempt at posing as a cupcake-hungry musician.

After second period, I straight-up blitzed him, hoping to catch him off-guard, but nope - that idea bombed, too.

It was weird, I spent all week trying NOT to get pranked by Gabe, and now I couldn't get him to do it no matter how bad I wanted it!

The same thing happened the rest of the afternoon, and by lunchtime, he STILL hadn't given me my fake cupcake.

I was starting to wonder if maybe I was wrong about the prank.

I mean, we all know I'm almost NEVER wrong about stuff, but it DOES happen.

Sometimes.

Anyways, after I grabbed my lunch, I rolled into the cafeteria with my Sneakys. The place was packed and louder than normal, almost like it was some kind of celebration.

I wasn't sure what the fuss was about until I saw Mr. Mitchell's "Happy 25th Anniversary" banner on the wall.

That's why everybody was partying. Because It WAS a party.

But it was the kind of party you'd expect teachers to have. You know - low-key, no loud music, no farm animals, no pyrotechnics - THAT kind of party.

In other words - lame.

You can't really blame teachers for that, though. It's just their nature.

Mr. Mitchell was under his banner, sporting a cone-shaped party hat with his arms crossed and his usual "I'm no fun" face which kinda looked like a frown, but also like he just smelled something absolutely wretched but couldn't figure out what it was.

I spotted my friends at a table across the room and started making my way over but stopped when I FINALLY saw it... Gabe and his cupcakes.

It was the prank I'd been waiting for all day. And look at that - Gabe even put a bow on top. Aww, he shouldn't have!

Gabe was walking right toward me, so I put my lunch tray down on the table next to me and waited patiently with my JUST deserts.

I smiled a big ol' gullible smile as he wheeled his cupcake cart down the aisle. He had no idea what was about to happen!

Things were about to get REAL.

At last, Gabe was right in front of me. I gotta say - his cupcakes LOOKED delish. He did a bang-up job of making them look so real! I put my hands on my hips, cocked my head with a smile, and said, "For me? Yum!"

But then he walked right past me and said...

Okay, hold up.

Gabe made a whole tray of pretend cupcakes that WEREN'T for me? Like, what in the heckin' heck was going on?? If they weren't for ME, then who were they for??

I watched Gabe wheel his dumb cupcakes all the way through the cafeteria until he stopped at Mr. Mitchell.

Gabe turned his head with a sly smile.

And then he winked. At ME.

OMG, he was gonna prank Mr. Mitchell!

Out of everybody at the school, Mr. Mitchell was the one who would've HATED it the most! That dude hates fun so much that getting popped by a cupcake might LITERALLY make his brain pop a vessel!

What an evil thing to do to that poor old man on his 25th year anniversary! Somebody had to do something, but I was the only person who knew what was happening!

If Gabe was gonna be stopped, it was only ME who could stop him. I'd have to run and make a huge scene, but I had a reason to do it, right?

That's when it suddenly hit me – stopping the prank would make me the HERO.

Mr. Mitchell's brain would remain unharmed, which meant I'd LITERALLY save his life! Students would cheer, Gabe would get busted, and I could make an awesome video out of it!

PLUS, Emma would see the whole thing because she was sitting close to Mr. Mitchell's banner. I mean, that had nothing to do with the situation, but it was still bonus points for me.

Gabe handed Mr. Mitchell a single cupcake. I sprang into action, racing down the aisle as fast as I could, but it wasn't fast enough.

Lucky for me, I was wearing Sneakys.

I shouted at the top of my lungs, leaned back on my heels, and let the hidden wheels do all the work.

SO happy I bought those things.

Mr. Mitchell was just about to take a bite when he froze at the sight of a super rad 6th grader comin' in hot. Gabe's fake cupcake was so close to Mr. Mitchell's mouth that the frosting was just skimming the dude's upper lip, like, gross!

I must've been going THIRTY, maybe FORTY miles per hour, or for my metric Fans, I must've been going a hundred, maybe TWO hundred kilometers per hour!

Whatever. All I'll say is that it was stupid fast. Like, WAY stupid fast. So fast that I couldn't stop.

I tried snatching the fake cupcake from Mr. Mitchell's hand, but since I was going at warp speed, I had to settle for slapping it away from him instead, which I totally did LIKE A BOSS.

After my successful saving of the day, I kept right on rolling until I pancaked against the brick wall under the banner.

I plopped onto to the floor and rolled to my back, waiting for my praise. Waiting to hear the chanting of my name. Waiting to be helped up and high-fived by pretty much everybody in there.

But... none of that noise happened.

Instead, there were gasps and hushed whispers. Some OMG's and Holy moly's.

Then I looked up at Mr. Mitchell's face and realized why nobody was cheering...

[intensity intensifies]

Instead of slapping the cupcake AWAY from Mr. Mitchell, I slapped it INTO Mr. Mitchell. There was frosting and ACTUAL CAKE all over his face!

There wasn't supposed to be ACTUAL CAKE! It was supposed to be FAKE, remember?? It was supposed to be a balloon covered in frosting – NO ACTUAL CAKE. So, was I wrong about Gabe's prank?? Was it even a prank at all??

The crowd of kids stared at me, shocked. Well, everybody except Gabe. He was holding back laughter.

Fergus and Dutch were there, too, ready to bust me again, and I could see it on Fergus' face – he was heartbroken.

That's when Principal Hawkins pushed through the shocked crowd and gasped, appalled at what I had done.

It was bad. REALLY bad.

My mouth started running. I told everybody the cupcake was supposed to be FAKE – that it was supposed to be a balloon that was gonna pop when Mr. Mitchell bit into it, but NOBODY believed me.

Principal Hawkins started coming toward me, and I panicked. I knew that ONE of Gabe's cupcakes from his tower had to be fake. All I had to do was prove it to everybody else and all would've been forgiven!

NONE of the cupcakes had a balloon in them. They were all legit. Every. Single. One. When it was over, I stood there in the slop of my own failures, staring at the floor when I suddenly heard a familiar phrase...

I couldn't believe it. Gabe PRETENDED to steal one of my ideas only to get me with ANOTHER stolen idea.

Had he been playing me all week??

Did he drop the frosting in front of me on purpose?? Did he keep cupcake mix in his locker because he knew I'd try to get in there? Did he place the cupcake liners and balloons in his videos because he knew that I'd spot them??

Hawkins didn't say a word. He just motioned for me to follow him. So, I did. I trudged through all the cake and frosting on the floor as students backed away. My friends watched sadly, but Fergus wouldn't even look at me.

I was done. That was it. Game over.

I was gonna be branded as the bad kid. My best friends wouldn't ever talk to me again. I could forget about ever asking Emma out. And my parents were gonna take my camera away, for sure.

I don't know if permanent records are real or not, but if they are, then the "Cupcake Incident" was definitely going in it. Someday, I'll try to buy a house, and the banker will flip to this section of my life and be like, "Oooo, looks like you DESTROYED an old man's party... sorry, we can't help you. Now, please leave before we call security."

When I finally caught up to Hawkins, we started walking toward the cafeteria doors. He'd probably call my mom or dad, and then one of them would have to leave work early to come pick me up, and then everything would just go from bad to worse.

My life was over.

Completely and totally over.

But that's when Mr. Mitchell called out to Principal Hawkins.

Both of us turned at the same time, and then...

Everybody in the cafeteria gasped so hard that the walls shook. Mr. Mitchell had just blasted Principal Hawkins with a crumbled-up ball of cake and frosting.

Like, whaaaaat??

The principal was silent. Dead-silent. Like, the kind of silent that's a little eerie. He smacked his lips, clearing some of the cupcake away from his mouth. Then, with his voice barely above a whisper, he said...

And that's when the most INSANE thing happened. If I hadn't caught it on camera then NOBODY would've believed it. Principal Hawkins grabbed some cupcake off of his face and my shirt, balled it up, and shouted...

The crowd went nuts.

EVERYBODY joined in.

Food went flying all over the place as kids screamed with laughter and joy.

I guess all it took for them to join a food fight was for the principal to start it. Who would'a thunk?

And while beautiful chaos unfolded in front of me, I happily stood back and caught the whole thing on my camera.

## EPISODE EIGHTEEN:
# TOO HOT TO HANDLE

Me! Duh!

The food fight didn't last long, maybe thirty seconds? When it was over, Mr. Mitchell and Principal Hawkins were laughing so hard that tears were coming out of their eyes.

Mr. Mitchell had FUN, and I got the epic food fight I'd always wanted. That's a TOTAL win/win, but honestly? I was just happy that Fergus wasn't mad at me again! Oh, and that Emma saw the whole thing, too. So, lotsa good stuff here.

The cafeteria was a sloppy disaster afterwards, but Hawkins didn't care. He said it was worth it to give Mr. Mitchell the epic 25th anniversary party he deserved.

I think the BEST part was that Mr. Mitchell STARTED it, like, who would've seen THAT coming?

I'm pretty sure that's the reason why I didn't get in trouble, but Hawkins never said, and I never asked.

When everything calmed down, I went straight to Gabe and called for a truce. I wanted to be DONE with prank videos.

Not for forever, but at least for a while.

I didn't expect Gabe to agree to the truce, but he surprised me again. He was actually super into it because all the hard work of making and editing videos every day and night was leaving him totally drained.

See, Gabe's problem was that he hit it too hard too fast. He burned himself out spending every waking second making and editing videos. CLASSIC rookie mistake. It's like my mom always says when we go to buffets...

The brutal truth is that it's hard work being a YouTuber, but that's not gonna stop ME.

I'll keep grinding until I finally make it to the top, and I promise you, I WILL MAKE IT TO THE TOP, even if I have to make 100 seasons of this stuff!

But until then, I'm gonna recharge my batteries by eating floor cupcakes and hanging out with people I love...

Download this FREE short comic adventure from www.MarcusEmerson.com when you sign up for his newsletter!

diary of a 6th grade ninja

short comic adventure

BY MARCUS EMERSON

What're you waiting for?? It's FREE!

Marcus Emerson is the author and illustrator of a whole lot of books including the way popular DIARY OF A 6TH GRADE NINJA series, THE SUPER LIFE OF BEN BRAVER series, and the SECRET AGENT 6th GRADER series. His goal is to ~~make money~~ create children's books that are funny and inspirational for kids of all ages - even the adults who never grew up.

Marcus still dreams of becoming an astronaut and WALKING ON THE SUN, LIKE WHAT?? THAT'S NOT EVEN POSSIBLE.

YET.

THANKS FOR READING! IF YOU LIKED THIS BOOK, CAN I ASK YOU TO HELP SPREAD THE WORD BY SHARING IT OR LEAVING AN HONEST REVIEW FOR IT? THANKS! YOU'RE AWESOME!